LITTLE
CLAM

by LYNN REISER

Greenwillow Books, New York

The endpaper design is adapted
from the American quilt pattern
"Ocean Waves."

Watercolor paints and a black pen were used
to create the full-color art. The text type is Helvetica.

Printed in Singapore by Tien Wah Press
First Edition   10 9 8 7 6 5 4 3 2 1

Library of Congress Cataloging-in-Publication Data
Reiser, Lynn.
Little clam / by Lynn Reiser.
      p.   cm.
Summary: After repeated warnings from his friends
at the edge of the sea, a little clam digs in with his
strong foot and succeeds in escaping the dangerous
predators who want to eat him.
ISBN 0-688-15908-7 (trade)
ISBN 0-688-15909-5 (lib. bdg.)
[1. Clams—Fiction.   2. Marine animals—Fiction.]
I. Title.   PZ7.R27745Li   1998   [E]—dc21
97-34511   CIP   AC

To the islands —
Susan and Bud's Ocracoke,
Susan's Monhegan,
and Lilibel's Sanibel

Once there

was a little clam

who lived in a shell

at the edge of the sea.

Every day
when the tide went out,
the little clam
pulled in his siphons,

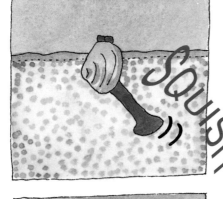
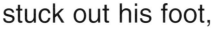

stuck out his foot,

and dug deep
under the sand.

Then
he pulled in his foot,

squeezed his shell shut,
and waited.

When the tide came in,
the little clam
stretched out his siphons
and slept under the sea.

One day the tide whispered,

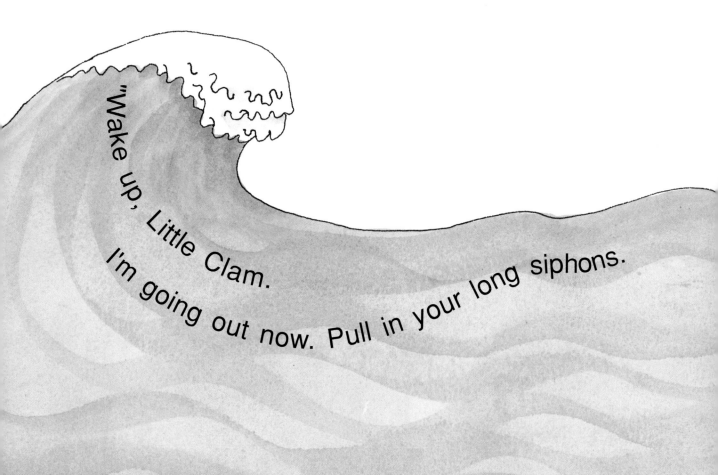

"Wake up, Little Clam. I'm going out now. Pull in your long siphons.

Stick out your strong foot. Dig, Little Clam."

The little clam was already awake.

But he was not listening.

He was busy swirling his siphons.

Far away, voices were calling.

Little Clam?

Little Clam?

Where are you?

Little Clam?

Where are you?

Where are you, Little Clam?

Where are you, Little Clam?

Where are you?

Little Clam?

Where are you, Little Clam?

A blue-eyed scallop flapped by and said,
"Little Clam, listen.
The hungry gull is looking for you.
The hungry conch is looking for you.
The hungry sea star is looking for you.
Pull in your long siphons.
Stick out your strong foot.
Dig, Little Clam."

But the little clam was not listening.
He was busy squirming in his shell.

Not very far away, the voices were calling,

There you are
There you are
There you are Little

A sideways crab
scuttled by and said,
"Little Clam, listen.
The hungry gull and
the hungry conch and
the hungry sea star
are watching you.
Pull in your long siphons.
Stick out your strong foot.
Dig, Little Clam."

But the little clam
was busy sifting sand.
He was not listening.

Not far away at all, voices were calling.

*Here we are
Little Clam,
and
we are*
**VERY
HUNGRY**

The little clam had finished
swirling and squirming and sifting.
Now he was ready to listen.

The sideways crab
and the blue-eyed scallop
were yelling,
"Listen, Little Clam!
The hungry gull
is reaching out its beak for you!
The hungry conch
is reaching out its foot for you!
The hungry sea star
is reaching out its arm for you!

"Pull in your long siphons.
Stick out your strong foot!
Dig, Little Clam, dig!"

The little clam just said,
"Oh.

"Thank you for telling me."

Then
quick—
the little clam
pulled in
his long siphons,
and squirted
the surprised gull,

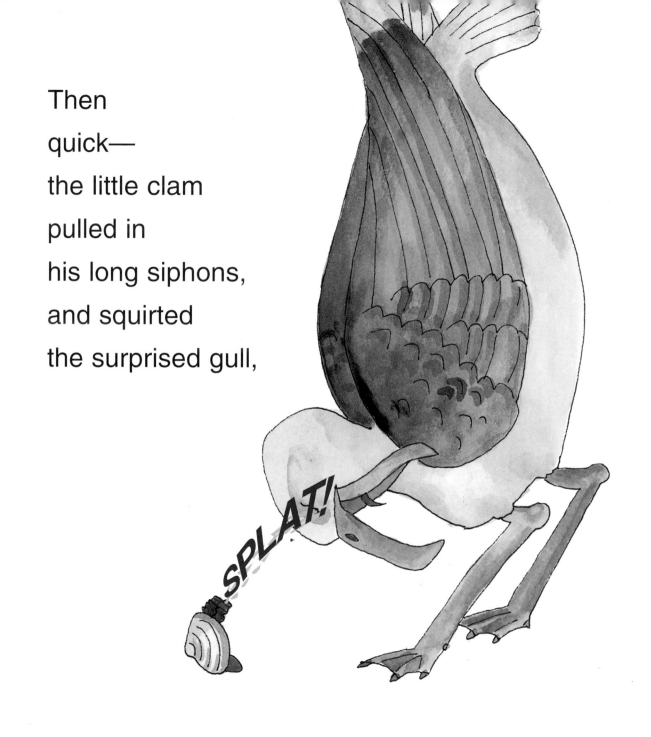

SPLAT!

SMACK!

stuck out
his strong foot,
and kicked
the startled conch,

pulled his foot in,
squeezed his shell shut,
and pinched
the shocked sea star.

SNAP!

The tide roared,

"Little Clam,
I am turning.
Little Clam,
I am coming in—"

And before the surprised gull
and the startled conch
and the shocked sea star could
remember that they were hungry,

the tide crashed in and drenched the gull, and flipped

the conch, and spun the sea star.

Then the tide
tucked the little clam under the sand
and covered him with her waves
and whispered,
"Listen, Little Clam.
Go to sleep.
Stick out your long siphons.
Pull in your strong foot.
Sleep, Little Clam.
The hungry gull cannot find you now.
The hungry conch cannot watch you now.
The hungry sea star cannot reach you now.
They are gone,
washed ashore by my waves."

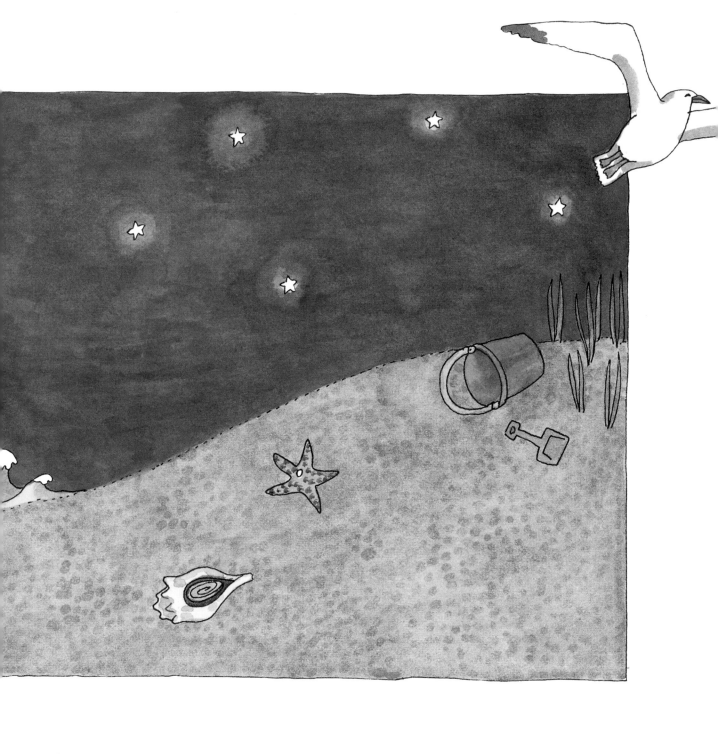

And the blue-eyed scallop
and the sideways crab
sang with the tide,

"Sleep, Little Clam, sleep.
The waves roll high above you.
The sand is snug around you.

Deep under the sea, safe under the sand,
dream, Little Clam, dream."

But the little clam was not listening.

He was already asleep.

Sleep tight, my little clam.

A LITTLE CLAM GAME

1. THE LITTLE CLAM

Siphons
Shell
Foot

2. SQUIRMING, SWIRLING, SIFTING

3. THE TIDE GOING OUT

4. THE TIDE TURNING

5. THE TIDE COMING IN

6. SLEEP TIGHT